TORTOISE
VS
HARE
THE REMATCH!

Written by
Preston Rutt

Illustrated by
Ben Redlich

START

meadowside
CHILDREN'S BOOKS

Now it's Saturday night.

It's time. Time to stop the chat and start the stopwatches. Time to learn who's the champ and who's the chump. Time for

Tortoise vs Hare
The Rematch
to begin!!!

Over to you, Cat Freeman, at trackside.

Cat Freeman: Thanks Jonny,
I'm here with Hare and Tortoise.
Hare, you've been training hard,
can you win back your crown?

Hare: *I'm good.*
Just too good for the wood.
I'm gonna make Tortoise look
like a Christmas pud.
There's only one runner should
rule this neighbourhood.
Understood?

Cat Freeman: Er...
thank you, Hare. Tortoise,
what do you say to that?

Tortoise: W–e–l–l...

Cat Freeman: Sorry,
Tortoise, I'll have to
stop you there. The race
is about to start.
Back to the studio!

START

And Tortoise is finally, ahem, into his...

...stride.

Whoops...

...a...

...daisy!

But wait!!

I don't believe it!

Tortoise has turned this race upside down.

Here comes the finish line. And it's oh so close!

Go, go, go...

Go crazy, folks!
We have a winner!

Ahem,
I said good night!

Excitement over.
Close your eyes now
please! Thank you.
Good night.

For Mum & Dad,
my champions

P.G.R.

For Jasmine
& Asher

B.R.

First published in 2010
by Meadowside Children's Books,
185 Fleet Street, London, EC4A 2HS
www.meadowsidebooks.com

Text © Preston Rutt 2010
Illustrations © Ben Redlich 2010

The rights of Preston Rutt
and Ben Redlich to be identified as
the author and illustrator of this
work have been asserted by them
in accordance with the Copyright,
Designs and Patents Act, 1988

A CIP catalogue record for this book
is available from the British Library

10 9 8 7 6 5 4 3 2 1

Printed in China